SOARING OVER THE TITANIC

BY SEAN PETRIE
ILLUSTRATED BY CARL PEARCE

Book design by Jake Slavik
Illustrations by Carl Pearce

Photographs ©: Library of Congress, 67; Tim Merry/N&S SYNDICATION/Express Newspapers/AP Images, 69

Published in the United States by Jolly Fish Press, an imprint of North Star Editions, Inc.

First Edition
First Printing, 2021

This is a work of fiction. Names, characters, places, and incidents are either the product of the author's imagination or are used fictitiously, and any resemblance to actual persons living or dead, business establishments, events, or locales is entirely coincidental.

Library of Congress Cataloging-in-Publication Data (pending)
978-1-63163-555-7 (paperback)
978-1-63163-554-0 (hardcover)

Jolly Fish Press
North Star Editions, Inc.
2297 Waters Drive
Mendota Heights, MN 55120
www.jollyfishpress.com

Printed in the United States of America

TABLE OF CONTENTS

CHAPTER 1

Jett Ryder tensed as the wave rolled toward his stand-up paddleboard.

His best friend Mika Moore cheered from her board nearby. "You got this, Jett!"

They were on Seattle's Elliott Bay. Both of them lived close by, and they had rented paddleboards with their families. Jett's parents were on their own boards, several yards back. Mika's mom had decided to watch the group from shore.

Jett leaned forward. The wave wasn't huge, but it was larger than anything they had encountered so far.

And it had appeared almost out of nowhere. Flecks of white foam leaped from the crest. Just before the wave hit, the front of Jett's board dipped. Then the sea pushed him toward the clouds.

"Whoa!" He wobbled backward, then sideways, then finally caught his balance. He glanced at Mika. "Pretty awesome, huh?"

She grinned. "Motocross daredevil, nearly taken out by a one-foot wave."

Jett returned her smile. He was the world's most famous motocross stunt rider. And at twelve years old, he was also the youngest. But this was his first time on a paddleboard.

The bigger wave was gone, but smaller ones still bobbed his board in a steady rhythm. "It feels like the ground is alive," Jett said. "It would be so cool to set up a ramp right here."

They were at least a hundred yards from the shore. Across the bay, the Seattle skyline looked like a giant key turned on its side, framed by the towering Cascade Mountains. A fresh breeze blew, carrying the salty tang of the ocean. All around, the dark, green water lapped at their boards.

"This far out," said Mika, "you'd need a massive stabilization system."

In addition to being Jett's best friend, Mika was

also a twelve-year-old engineering genius. She and her team designed all of Jett's stunts.

Jett nodded. "But just imagine it: riding across the sea, then leaping into the sky!"

A loud splashing startled them both. Jett's dad had arrived on his paddleboard. "A water stunt?" He sat down on his board and clapped his hands together, like a seal asking for a treat. "Tell me more, tell me more!"

He made a honking noise, then grinned. Jett's dad could charm the brine from a barnacle. He was also one of Jett's co-managers.

A second later, Jett's mom zipped by on her

paddleboard, gliding across the waves like she was part fish.

"Jett's going to jump his bike in the water!" his dad called to her.

Jett's mom was his other co-manager. She let her paddle trail in the waves and did a slow turn until she came to a stop, facing Jett. "Last I checked, motocross bikes don't float. What exactly is your father talking about?"

Jett knew that every stunt was a push-pull balance between his parents. His dad always went for glitz and glamor. His mom was the voice of reason and reality.

"We were thinking of doing a stunt out here," Jett said. "If we had a floating track and ramp, it would look like I'm riding across the bay. Then I could do a jump."

His dad let out a whoop. *"Jett Ryder Rides on Water*! Our sponsors will drink that up!"

"After the jump, where will you land?" his mom asked.

"On another floating ramp?" Jett offered.

They all looked to Mika. She thought a moment, then shook her head. "You saw how fast that bigger wave formed, Jett. Putting one ramp this far out would be difficult at best. Having two of them here would make the jump more unpredictable than we could manage."

"Crowds love unpredictable!" said Jett's dad.

But Jett never did a stunt unless he was absolutely sure he could perform it safely. And there was no one he trusted with those decisions more than Mika. Except perhaps his mom.

"If it's too risky," Jett said, "then we won't do it."

His mom nodded. "We don't want your bike ending up as the next wreck at the bottom of Elliott Bay."

"There aren't any shipwrecks here," said Jett's dad. "They're in the ocean."

"Actually," said Mika, "there are sunken ships in

bays and rivers and lakes all over. There are at least five beneath us right now. Hardly anyone remembers them, though." In addition to being an engineering whiz, Mika was also a major history buff.

Jett's dad gave her a confused look, then stuck his head under the murky, green water. He came up a few seconds later, his hair and beard dripping. "I didn't see any."

They all laughed.

Jett watched the sun glitter across the water's surface. The bay looked like it was covered in sparkling jewels. "There's got to be a water stunt we can do." He thought of the ships hidden below the shiny waves, buried in darkness. "What if we did something to honor the wrecks? All those people who've been forgotten."

"A tribute stunt," said his dad. "That's a great idea. As long as it's big enough."

"And safe enough," said his mom.

Jett felt the bay rise and fall beneath him, like it was nodding in agreement.

CHAPTER 2

"Are there really five ships down there?" Jett asked. He took a bite of fish and chips. They had returned the paddleboards and joined Mika's mom in a small restaurant overlooking Elliott Bay.

Mika nodded. "One of them was the worst wreck in Seattle's history."

"It was?"

Mika got a faraway look. "In November 1906, a passenger ship called the *Dix* was crossing Elliott Bay. A mile out, it struck another ship and sank within minutes. Thirty-nine people went down with it."

"What about treasure?" asked Jett's dad. "Are there any gold coins down there? We could do a stunt—and retrieve some loot at the same time!"

"If there was something valuable," said Mika's mom, "you'd have to jump through a lot of maritime law hoops to claim it." Mika's mom was an attorney, and she handled all the paperwork for Jett's stunts.

"Those aren't the kind of jumps I want to do," said Jett.

"Me either," said his dad. "Okay, no treasure. But we still need a water-stunt idea."

"What about something close to shore?" asked Jett's mom. "Like a jump from land to water."

Mika nodded. "Other stunt performers have jumped from a pier onto a barge. And leaped a bike between two barges near the shore. Both of those are doable."

"And have already been *done*," said Jett's dad. "Our sponsors don't want a repeat. They want something new."

Jett pointed to the window. "But if we did a jump by the shore, dedicated to Seattle's biggest shipwreck, that would be new. Once the water was calmer, of course."

Outside, the wind had picked up. The bay was filled with large waves and bursts of whitecaps.

His dad took a bite of fries, like he was chewing the idea over. Then he shook his head. "That wreck still isn't enough to draw a large crowd. I'd never even heard of it until today. We need something more."

Out on the turbulent bay, a massive container ship inched its way toward Puget Sound. It was the length of a football field and piled high with huge metal boxes. Beside it, a passenger ferry bobbed on the rough waters. The container ship looked like a floating mountain—it made the ferry seem like a matchbox. Jett sighed. His Elliott Bay idea was like the ferry. They needed a stunt the size of a container ship.

"What are some other big wrecks?" he asked Mika.

"Well, there's the *Titanic*, of course."

"Now we're talking!" said Jett's dad.

"That's in the middle of the Atlantic Ocean," said

Jett's mom. "That's basically the opposite of safe and stable."

"There are some right by the coast," said Mika. "The *Princess Sophia* was the largest shipwreck of the Northwest, and it's off the Alaskan shore. When it sank, newspapers called it 'the Unknown *Titanic*.'"

"I like that," said Jett's dad. "Except for the unknown part."

"What happened with the *Princess Sophia*?" asked Jett.

"It was a popular travel ship between Alaska and Seattle," said Mika. "The captain had sailed the route hundreds of times. But he got caught in a blizzard and hit a reef at 3:00 a.m. in icy waters. At least four hundred thirty people were on board. None of them survived."

Jett shuddered at the thought.

"I can't believe I've never heard of these wrecks," said his mom.

"You can't really put a marker in the water to remember them," explained Mika. "And there aren't any relics, unless someone dives down and finds them. There are passenger ships, warships, and of course all the early explorers, at the bottom of seas all over the world."

Jett's dad nodded. "A stunt at the *Princess Sophia*

site would draw a better crowd, but still not the size we're looking for. Most likely, only people around here would know about it."

"What about a wreck outside of this area?" Jett asked.

"There's the *Sultana* in Tennessee," said Mika. "Worst ship disaster in US history."

Everyone scooted their chairs closer to the table. Maybe this was the one.

"It was 1865," said Mika. "The Civil War had just ended. The *Sultana* was a steamship on the Mississippi River, and it was overloaded with passengers. Most were soldiers from the Union army who had been captured during the war, but were now being freed and sent home. A boiler on the ship exploded, and the ship went down. Over eighteen hundred people were lost."

Jett's dad let out a low whistle. "That's a big one for sure." He sat back in his chair and crossed his arms. "But I still don't think it's well-known enough to get a large enough audience."

Jett threw up his hands. "Dad, that's the whole point—to *get* people to remember!"

"I know, Jett. I want that, too." His dad looked at him calmly and put his hand on Jett's shoulder. "But we need something big for people to pay attention.

Once we have that, *then* we can dedicate the stunt to the smaller wrecks. We use the big stuff to help remember the rest."

Jett started to protest, but deep down, he knew his dad was right.

"We need a stunt that's different from what's already been done," his dad continued. "Or one that's centered around a more famous event. That could do the trick."

Outside, the waves tumbled angrily across Elliott Bay. They looked like Jett felt. He thought of all the forgotten shipwrecks, and all the adventurers and travelers, the soldiers and explorers, who'd been aboard. More than ever, he wanted to do a stunt for them. He just didn't know how.

CHAPTER 3

Jett sped across the dirt. He revved his bike engine, and it let out a joyful *braaap*. He was at their practice field in the country. He still had no idea what to do for the water stunt. But he knew the best way to clear his head.

The air whistled in his helmet as the field flashed by. Mika and his parents were at the far edge, still discussing stunt possibilities. As Jett raced away from them, his bike thrummed with power, vibrating so much it seemed to shake his bones.

Some riders liked the smoother four-stroke

engines, but Jett preferred the raw burst of the two-stroke engine. With a two-stroke, he felt more in touch with his bike and the terrain underneath.

Right now he felt the pure speed of racing over the flat field. But that was about to change. Up ahead were the whoops. Jett smiled and went into attack position.

His bike jostled and jolted as he hit the whoops, keeping himself loose and centered on the bike. That was the key to the whoops—to any unpredictable spot, really—to ride with it, not through it.

Jett skimmed the whoops in a teeth-chattering rhythm, like the two of them were doing a series of

high-fives. He imagined doing the same thing on the waves, racing his bike across the rolling surface of Elliott Bay.

He let out a *whoop!* of his own as the bumps finished. Then he angled his bike toward the best part of the track: the main jump ramp.

The ground was smooth again as Jett twisted the throttle wide open. The world blurred and his heart picked up in time with his speed. At the base of the ramp, he pushed down through the pegs and rode upward.

And then he was soaring!

The air seemed to part for him like a swishing

curtain. To the sides, it tugged playfully at his gloves, almost like the air was trying to catch a ride. And below, the wind raced beneath his wheels in an excited rush.

While Jett enjoyed the whoops, he *lived* for jumping.

He was almost at the high point of the jump. Mika liked to draw out each jump on paper, calculating the angle and speed. But Jett did it more by instinct. Somehow, he just *knew* what he needed to do for each one.

He wondered if ship captains did that, too. Sure, they had all sorts of charts and maps. But sometimes, did they just *feel* their way through the water—like he did with the air?

At the crest of the jump, Jett imagined he was above the middle of Elliott Bay. He pictured the waves dancing with delight as he soared over.

Then he felt the tug of gravity. Jett focused on the practice field again, locking onto the landing ramp in the dirt below. Just before he hit, he angled the front of his bike downward to match the slope of the ramp. He landed perfectly, with both tires making contact at the same time.

Jett wished he could have done the jump over Elliott Bay for real. But Mika had said it would be too unstable that far out. He remembered the ferry he'd seen bobbing in those rough waves—and then he nearly fell off his bike.

There *was* a way to do a jump over deeper water. Of course!

He sped to the far edge of the practice field to tell Mika and his parents.

"A container ship jump!" Jett said breathlessly as he took off his helmet.

"Those are definitely big," said his dad, looking interested.

Jett caught his breath and turned to Mika. "You said before that we needed something massively stable in order to do a jump over the middle of the bay, right?"

"I did."

"When we were in the fish and chips restaurant, those big waves were bouncing a passenger ferry up and down. But they didn't do a thing to a container ship—it just kept plodding along. Steady and level."

A glimmer of understanding appeared in Mika's eyes.

"If we had *two* of them," Jett said, "we could put a jump ramp on one . . . and a landing ramp on the other."

Mika nodded. "Container ships are built to stay

extremely stable in rough water, to keep the cargo from falling off. In theory, we could put two in the middle of the bay and jump between them."

"Or," Jett said, "we could put two in the middle of the Atlantic Ocean." He paused to let it sink in. "Where the *Titanic* went down."

His dad let out a thundering clap. "Yes!"

Jett's mom furrowed her brow. "That's very different than doing a jump in Elliott Bay."

"The conditions can be a lot rougher," agreed Mika. "But if we had good weather and calm seas, a container ship in the ocean should be just as stable as one in the bay."

"If Jett fell in the water from high up," said his mom, "it would be like hitting concrete. Can we put a crash pit in the ocean?"

"Probably not," answered Mika. "Or at least not a very effective one. But container ship decks stay fairly low to the waterline. I'd say fifty feet or less above water."

"I've done higher jumps than that without a crash pit," Jett said. "And I would wear a life jacket as part of my stunt suit."

His mom crossed her arms, but she didn't say anything.

Jett knew she was leaning toward yes.

"A jump over the *Titanic* wreck site!" said his dad. "Now *that's* a stunt that could draw the kind of crowd we need!"

A thought struck Jett. "How big was the *Titanic*?"

Mika took out her phone and did a search. "At the middle of the main deck, it was ninety-two feet wide. When it set sail, the deck was about sixty feet above the waterline."

"What are you thinking, Jett?" his dad asked.

"If I did a jump bigger than that, it would be like I was leaping over the actual ship. We could call it *Soaring Over the* Titanic!"

His dad danced in place.

"A water jump will be extremely difficult," said his mom. "There are just so many variables that could go wrong."

"I'll practice till perfect like always, Mom. If it's not safe enough, I won't do it."

"And I won't let him," said Mika.

Jett made his final pitch: "This stunt will actually get the attention we need. For all the lesser-known wrecks."

His mom was silent. She never lost touch with reality, but she wanted a spectacular jump, too. "Okay," she finally said. Then she smiled. "I'm on board."

Jett grinned and held a hand up for Mika. "Get set . . ."

She gave him a fist bump in return. ". . . for Jett!"

CHAPTER 4

The stunt was a go. Mika's mom had received permission to do the jump at the spot where the *Titanic* went down. And Jett's dad had convinced their sponsors to secure two container ships.

Jett spent the next several days practicing.

First, Mika and her team calculated the dimensions. To simulate jumping over the *Titanic*, the container ships would be one hundred fifty feet apart, and Jett would leap seventy feet high. Both distances were well within his range. On land.

Next, they built a set of ramps at the practice field,

replicating the length and height of the container-ship leap. Jett did the jump over and over, until it felt as natural as shifting gears on his bike.

Now, it was time to try the water.

They were still waiting on the container ships to arrive, but Mika's mom had secured two barges near the Elliott Bay shore. They put ramps on each one—a jumping barge and a landing barge. Then, to start small, they anchored the barges fifty feet apart.

Jett double-checked the clasps on his life jacket, then kick-started his bike to life. He rode a few laps around the deck of the jumping barge. Sometimes it felt like riding on the ground. Other times it would

dip or rise out of nowhere. His nerves were doing

the same.

Jett aimed his bike toward the ramp. He reminded

himself that this jump would be a piece of cake on

land. And the bay was calm, with just a few tiny

waves. He revved the engine and shot forward.

The deck was swaying, but Jett rode through it, gripping the handlebars as tight as he could. Just before the base of the ramp, the deck began to bob sharply. It felt like riding over a patch of shifting, squishy whoops.

Jett gritted his teeth and fought against the movement. He shot up the ramp, the same way he'd done hundreds of times on the ground.

But at the edge, the barge pitched downward. Jett soared up, but the push-off from the ramp had felt awkward and weak.

As he flew over the water, Jett struggled to keep his bike aimed upward. The air didn't have the same joyful feel as usual. Instead, it felt like the air was hanging on for dear life.

Jett focused on the landing barge. Gravity was yanking him down fast.

He had just enough distance to make it. He angled his bike to match the downward slope of the ramp. Then, right when he thought he might be okay, the barge suddenly surged upward.

Jett's front tire hit too soon. The back of his bike bucked, like it was trying to fling him off. Jett fought to stay on, but he was thrown over the handlebars. He tumbled off the bike and rolled all the way down the ramp.

Thankfully, the barge was long enough that Jett came to a stop before falling overboard.

A second later, his mom was at his side. No matter where or how he wrecked, his mom was always the first one there.

"Jett, are you hurt? Is anything broken?" His mom scanned him to see if anything seemed seriously hurt.

His head was ringing and his wrists were sore, but he felt intact. Other than his heart thumping a hundred miles an hour. "I don't think so."

His mom breathed a sigh of relief.

Jett started to sit up, but his mom placed a hand on the center of his chest.

Normally, Jett would have pushed himself to his feet and said he was fine. But as he lay there, he felt his heartbeat calming.

It reminded him of the very first time he'd ridden a bike. Not a motocross bike, but a BMX, when he was very young. He'd been wobbly and afraid. When he hit a big bump, he'd toppled sideways and struck the ground hard.

His mom had rushed over and put her hand on his chest, just like she was doing now. After he'd sat up, she'd rocked him back and forth for a few moments. Then he'd stood on his own, climbed back on the bike, and rode again—steady and sure.

"What happened out there?" his mom asked.

Beneath him, the waves rocked the barge back and forth.

"The ramp bucked up. I couldn't ride through it."

"Of course you couldn't. It's just like going over the whoops."

"But those are on the ground."

"When the ground is unpredictable, what do you do to stay stable?"

"Keep loose and centered," Jett answered immediately.

"Exactly." His mom pointed to the waves. "Remember the paddleboard? You tensed when that

47

big wave came. But you can't fight the water any more than you can fight the land. You have to ride *with* it, not through it. Like the two of you are doing a dance. Like this."

Suddenly his mom got up and made a wild, flailing motion with her arms. Jett laughed.

She held out a hand for him to join.

Jett stayed put. He was twelve years old. No way was he about to start dancing on a deck with his mom.

But she just stood there, a goofy grin on her face, one hand held out, waiting. Her arm swayed in time with the waves. Finally, Jett reached up and took hold.

And, for a few seconds, he let his mom twirl him

across the deck. Then they both let go at the same

time.

Jett was smiling as big as she was. He walked across the deck to retrieve his bike. The waves were still rocking the barge, but Jett didn't feel unsteady anymore.

CHAPTER 5

It was stunt day.

After his wreck, Jett had done the barge jump over and over. When the waves came, he'd gone with them rather than fighting them. He'd practiced until it felt almost as natural as doing it on land.

Then, when the container ships arrived, Jett had jumped between those. He'd started with a smaller leap, then increased the distance until he was able to do the full stunt. He'd practiced till perfect.

But that was all in Elliott Bay, with the shore in sight.

Now, they were in the middle of the Atlantic Ocean. Over the same spot where the *Titanic* had gone down.

It had taken several days to get there. And they'd had to wait several more for the weather to clear and the seas to calm. But today, the sky was cloudless. And the ocean looked like a sheet of glass.

A group of small boats floated nearby. Some were crammed with spectators. Others housed TV and media crews. Overhead, drones buzzed in the air, ready to capture Jett's leap on video. Two rescue boats patrolled the water, ready just in case.

Jett was on the first container ship, the one with

the jump ramp. Crowds lined the track that led to the ramp at the front of the ship's deck. A hundred fifty feet across the ocean, the container ship with the landing ramp sat waiting.

"Ready?" Mika asked in Jett's headset. She was on the landing ship, positioned at the top of its command tower so she could see the entire stunt.

"Always," answered Jett.

A second later, his dad's voice boomed from a set of speakers: "Welcome, friends and fans!" The crowds cheered. Jett's dad continued: "The sky is clear. The ocean is calm. And Jett Ryder is ready . . . to *Soar Over the* Titanic!"

Jett kick-started his bike and rode a few loops around the starting point. The deck beneath him felt steady and level.

"Today," his dad announced, "we'll witness history being made—and remembered!" He went on to describe how Jett would jump the dimensions of the *Titanic*, over the spot where it sank. "And while everyone remembers its story, this stunt is dedicated to the countless other wrecks filled with countless people whose tales have slipped beneath the waves and from memory. The ones who suffered the same fate, but not the same fame. Today Jett Ryder soars . . . for the forgotten!"

The crowds whooped and applauded. Jett rode his bike to the starting point and did his signature move—a double donut. He put one foot on the ground and rode around it in a circle, then switched to the other foot and did the same thing.

He'd done the move at the start of his very first jump. That time, it was just to steady his nerves. And then he'd done it after, when he'd successfully completed the jump. Since then, he'd done it at the start and finish of every stunt.

"And now," announced his dad. "Get set . . . for Jett!"

Both container ships sounded their deep,

bone-shaking horns. All the other boats did the same. Jett revved his engine and raced toward the jump ramp.

Beneath him, the deck swayed slightly. Jett thought of how massive the container ship was—and how much force it took to move the ship like that.

He twisted the throttle. The crowds lining the track blurred as he sped past. He imagined all the forgotten faces from all those other wrecks.

Then he focused on the jump ramp ahead.

"Jett!" Mika's voice sounded in his headset. "Jett, a huge wave just formed behind your ship. It's coming right toward you!"

There was no time to stop. Jett was going so fast that if he hit the brakes now he would either lose control or go up the ramp too slowly. Either way, he would almost certainly end up flying over the edge and plunging into the ocean below.

He went full throttle toward the jump ramp.

The wave hit his ship. The whole world seemed to pitch and roll as the horizon shifted higher. Jett felt the deck rise beneath him. A surge of panic also rose in his chest.

He gripped the handlebars as hard as he could. But then he heard his mom's words: "Ride with it, not against it. It's a dance."

Jett forced himself to stay loose and centered, just like on the whoops. Beneath him, the wave pushed everything higher. And he went with it.

He rode the steep ramp upward. The container ship began to pitch down, and Jett let his bike do the same. He moved with the motion of the ship and pushed off the edge of the ramp at the same time. He imagined he was jumping not just from the ship, but from the wave itself.

And then he soared into the air.

The horizon stretched in every direction. Below, he knew the wave was rolling along with him—like the two of them were racing across the empty ocean.

But Jett knew the ocean wasn't empty. Deep below the surface was the giant, rusting hull of the *Titanic*. He pictured himself sailing over it. Pictured its deck filled with people, faces turned up and watching.

Sooner than he expected, gravity pulled at his bike.

With a start, Jett realized he was descending too quickly.

The other container ship loomed ahead, its side a sheer wall of metal. If he hit it, he would tumble into the freezing water below. He had come here to honor all the victims—but what if he ended up becoming one?

He thought of them: the passengers and soldiers, the adventurers and explorers, all forgotten forever beneath the water.

But no, not forever.

He was here now to remember them. And help others remember them. And just like the *Titanic* passengers, he imagined they were all looking up and watching. And cheering.

Jett shook off the panic and focused on the landing ahead. He had to clear the container ship's side railing, then come down on the ramp.

The massive steel wall rushed toward him. At the last second, Jett used all his strength to lift the front of his bike.

He cleared the railing!

A second later, he slammed onto the landing ramp. But the wave had struck at the same time, swaying the huge ship upward.

Jett wobbled and struggled to keep his bike under control. If he crashed here, he could still go sailing off the side of the ship.

But as the wave rolled beneath, Jett relaxed the tiniest bit—and let his bike roll with it. Like he was riding along with the wave. Like a dance, in the middle of the ocean.

Then the wave passed, and the deck leveled. He had made it!

Jett brought his bike to a slow stop and did his signature double-donut move. Horns sounded in triumph from every boat on the water. The crowds went wild.

"Jett!" said Mika in his headset. "That was absolutely amazing! You should have seen it from up here!"

But Jett wasn't looking up. He gave a tip of his helmet to the endless ocean below.

"We won't forget you," he said. "Ever."

FOCUS ON
THE TITANIC

EPIC DISASTER

In 1912, the RMS *Titanic* was the largest ship in the world. On April 10, it departed from Southampton, England, for its very first voyage. It was carrying more than 2,200 people and headed to New York. Four days later, just before midnight in the lonely waters of the North Atlantic Ocean, it struck an iceberg. The impact ripped a hole in the ship's hull. Within a few hours, the world's biggest ship sank. Approximately 700 people boarded lifeboats and survived. But more than 1,500 people, including the captain, went down with the *Titanic* into the ocean depths.

DEEP DISCOVERY

The *Titanic* remained hidden for more than 70 years. In 1985, the ship was found in a joint mission between France and the United States. It was approximately 370 miles

(595 km) off the coast of Newfoundland. The *Titanic*'s wreckage remains on the ocean floor more than 12,400 feet (3,800 m) below the surface. Thousands of relics from the *Titanic* are now displayed in museums all over the world.

VANISHING REMAINS

Since the *Titanic*'s discovery, several groups have explored its wreckage. Video of the ship has revealed that it is rusting and falling apart. Deep-sea bacteria is one reason why. The wreck has also been underwater for more than 100 years. Over time, water breaks down metal. In 2019, some scientists believed that the *Titanic* could completely disappear by 2049.

THAT'S AMAZING!

TRAVIS PASTRANA'S BARGE-TO-BARGE BACKFLIP

In the world of motocross stunts, few can match Travis Pastrana. He has won multiple freestyle championships. As a tribute to his hero, Evel Knievel, Pastrana did three jumps that Knievel was never able to complete: leaping over fifty-two cars, then sixteen buses, and finally a fountain at Caesars Palace in Las Vegas—all in one day. He has even leaped from an airplane without a parachute.

But none of those stunts were his scariest ever.

Pastrana said his scariest stunt was on the River Thames in London in 2017. His team set up ramps on two barges. The barges were 75 feet (23 m) apart. And they were floating freely, not anchored or tied down. Pastrana's stunt? Leaping his motocross bike over the water from one barge to the other, while doing a backflip.

The day of the stunt, morning rains swept in, and winds reached 20 miles per hour (32 km/h).

With cameras rolling, Pastrana rode a few laps around

the first barge. Then he revved his bike and raced up the ramp. Just like Jett, his takeoff was rocky, and he thought he wouldn't make it. But he soared above the water, did a perfect backflip, and nailed the landing on the second barge.

Afterward, Pastrana said the waves moved each barge unpredictably. That made the stunt far more difficult than it looked.

GLOSSARY

attack position

The main motocross riding position for increasing speed and approaching jumps. The rider is standing, bending forward at the waist, knees slightly bent, elbows high, and looking forward.

BMX

Short for "bicycle motocross."

donut

A move where a rider puts one foot down and spins the bike around while riding in place, creating a circle on the ground.

four-stroke engine

A type of engine that tends to use less fuel and is quieter than a two-stroke engine, but is heavier and usually cannot work upside down.

freestyle

A type of motocross event where riders compete by doing tricks and jumps.

kick-started

Started an engine by stepping down on the bike's lever.

motocross

Off-road dirt bike racing, usually done on dirt tracks with jumps.

pegs

Short metal bars that extend at foot level on either side of a motocross bike, which a rider can use for support.

revved

Increased engine speed.

throttle

A twistable grip on the dirt bike's right handlebar, which can be turned to increase or decrease engine power.

two-stroke engine

A type of engine that tends to use more fuel and is louder than a four-stroke engine, but is lighter and can work upside down.

whoops

A section of motocross track made up of a series of dirt bumps. When a rider goes over these bumps by just barely touching the top of each one, it is called "skimming the whoops."

wide open

When the throttle is turned to increase engine power to its maximum.

ABOUT THE AUTHOR

Sean Petrie writes books for kids, including *Welders on the Job* and *Crash Corner*. He also writes poetry, usually on the spot on a 1928 Remington typewriter. His poetry books include *Typewriter Rodeo* and the Seattle-based *Listen to the Trees*. He lives in Austin, Texas.

ABOUT THE ILLUSTRATOR

Carl Pearce lives in north Wales with his wife, Ceri. When not lost in his illustration work, he enjoys watching films, reading books, and taking long walks along the beach. He graduated from the North Wales School of Art and Design as an illustrator. His first book was published on his graduation day in 2004. He has since gone on to illustrate countless books for children.